For my mother

Atheneum Books for Young Readers
An imprint of Simon & Schuster Children's Publishing Division
1230 Avenue of the Americas
New York, New York 10020

Book design by Kristin Smith
The text of this book is set in StempelSchneidler.
The illustrations are rendered in gouache and pen-and-ink.
Manufactured in China
2 4 6 8 10 9 7 5 3
Library of Congress Cataloging-in-Publication Data
Schwartz, Amy.
A glorious day / Amy Schwartz—1st ed.
p.   cm.
"A Richard Jackson Book."
Summary: Describes a day in the life of the children, animals, parents,
and baby-sitters in a small red brick apartment building.
[1. Neighbors—Fiction. 2. Apartment houses—Fiction. 3. Day—Fiction.]
ISBN 0-689-84802-1
PZ7 .S406 Gl 2004
[E]—dc21   2003003626

Morning

One baby, two little girls, three big boys,
four little boys, two cats, and a bird live in a
small apartment building made of red brick.
They are all early risers.

Henry is the first up. After he's been
up awhile and it's starting to get light out,
he hears Peter and Thomas upstairs.

Then Baby Susannah
and her two brothers get up.
Next the triplets and Will.

Henry eats a plum for breakfast and
a few noodles and one bite of hot dog.
Henry's bird nibbles on seeds.

"Hi, Princess," Henry says.
"Want to fly?"
He opens the cage door.

All the other kids are eating breakfast too. Cheerios, Rice Chex, baby cereal, and potato chips.

And then everybody starts getting dressed. Henry
decides to get dressed outside. On the stoop Henry's
mother helps him put on his diaper and long pants
and green shirt and shoes.

Thomas and Peter take the trash out with their dad.

"Look at Peter's lovely underpants," Henry's mother says.

"Henry wear underpants sooner or later," Henry says.

Baby Susannah's sitter comes into the building.
The triplets' auntie comes to watch them. Baby Susannah's
two brothers come out with their mother and pick up Will
for school.

Henry waves to the garbage man. He watches a shiny
blue car get towed.

The small red brick building is warm in the sun.

The day has begun.

Day

Henry runs up and down the steps of the small
red brick building ten times. Then he and his mother
walk to the grocery store.

Peter and Thomas are there too.
The mothers buy macaroni,
graham teddies, bananas, milk,
and ravioli.

Henry mails a letter on the
way back.

At home Henry and his mother play trains. Henry is the big train and his mother is the small train.
All morning long.

The kids in the building rattle rattles, paint pictures,

and jump on the sofa.

The mailman delivers the mail. Henry's mother goes into the hall to check the mailbox, and Princess flies out the door.

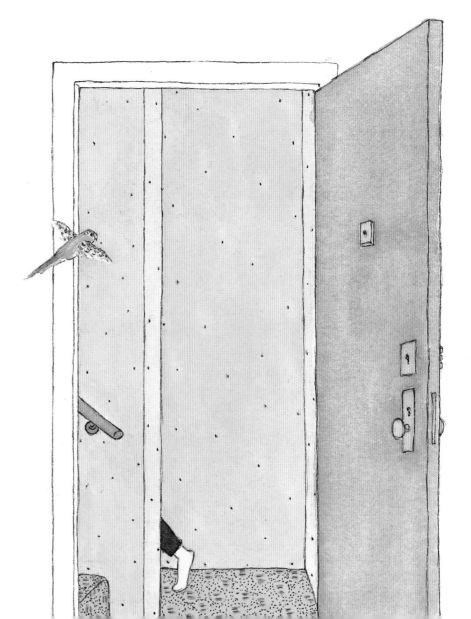

princess!

Henry and his mother search upstairs and downstairs, upstairs and down.

"Princess! Princess!"

Peter and Thomas and the triplets look too.

They find Princess at the top of the top staircase.

Henry's mother gets the cage, and Princess flies in.

"Never a dull moment," Henry's mother says.

For lunch the triplets go out for pizza.

Peter and Thomas have bagels with cream cheese,

and Henry has one bite of a number of things.

After lunch Henry lies down for a nap. All the
other kids are falling asleep too.

UPS comes and goes. A jackhammer starts and stops
out on the street. Henry's mother closes her eyes and
inside the small red apartment building everything
is still.

Until Henry wakes up.
And Baby Susannah and Peter
and Thomas and the triplets.
The mothers and sitters
make snacks and pack diaper bags
and put kids in sweaters.

Doors of apartments open
and close and the front door
of the red brick building swings
open and shut.
Everyone is leaving for
the playground.

Kids come in strollers,
on bikes, and in running shoes.
They bring balls and dolls and trucks.
Baby Susannah flies high in the swing.

The triplets ride in a parade and crash into one another's bikes. Henry finds sticks and puts them down the storm drain.

A breeze curls around the playground and floats back to the small red building. Kids come and go and laugh and yell and fall down and get up again.

It is a glorious afternoon.

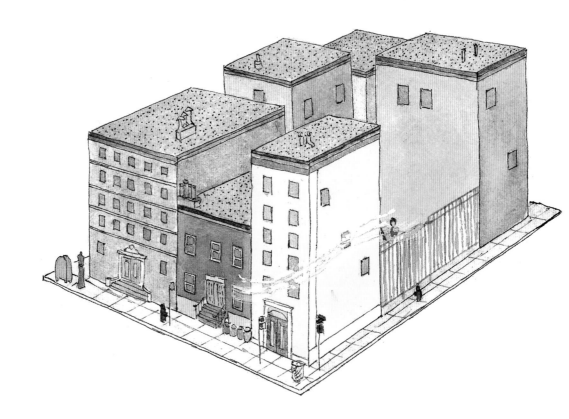

Night

In front of the small red building Peter and Thomas are drawing trains with colored chalk. When Henry gets home from the playground he adds smoke. He can hear Princess inside singing with the birds outside.

Soon the triplets are back too. The big boys come home from floor hockey and play on the sidewalk.

A neighbor walks by.

"Is this a school or something?" she asks.

The triplets' mother comes home and Baby Susannah's mother gets out of a cab and one by one the dads come home too. A pizza is delivered.

"Peter and Thomas! Time to go in!"

"Will! Let's go!"

It is dusk and one by one everybody goes inside.

The mothers and dads make dinner. The kids ride trucks, watch videos, and whoop and holler.

For dinner the kids
eat hamburgers, pizza,

chicken and corn,
and spaghetti and meatballs.

Princess pecks at a piece of lettuce.
Henry lines up all his green beans like a train.
Then he puts them in his orange juice.
"Bath time," Henry's mother says.

Henry can hear Peter and Thomas splashing upstairs.
Hot water and cold water are rushing through pipes
and into tubs all over the small red building. Kids play
with boats and ducks and pour water on the bathroom floor.

Soon the mothers and dads
take out big towels, and dry faces
and tummies and arms and legs.
Then the kids get into pj's and
it's time for bed.

Henry listens to *The Three Bears* five times. He
tells Dad about Princess.

Baby Susannah cries and her father rocks her.
Kids hear stories and tell stories and listen to songs.
They get tucked in with blankets and bears and
rabbits and trains. Henry asks for his red garbage truck.

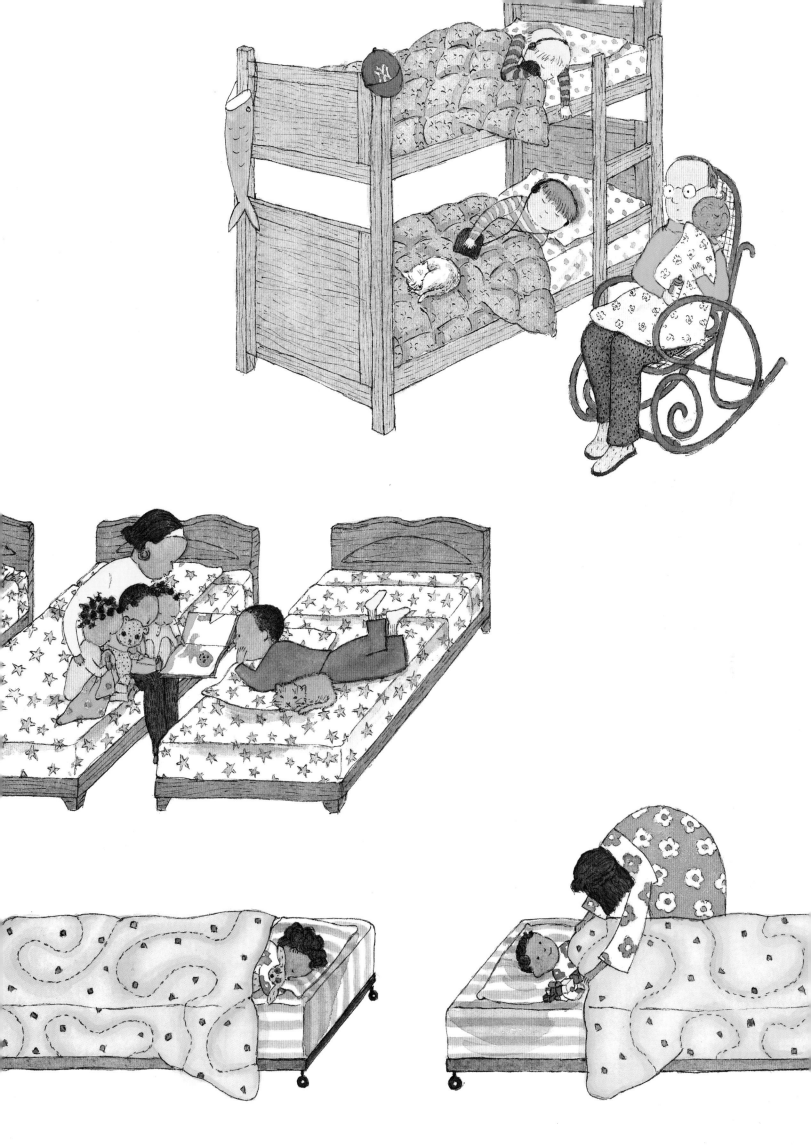

The moon comes up. And in a small apartment
building made of red brick, one baby, two little girls,
three big boys, four little boys, two cats, and a
bird fall fast asleep.

To Harry and Jenny

Anancy and Mr. Dry-Bone is an original story based on traditional characters from Caribbean and African folktales.

First North American Edition

First published in Great Britain in 1991 by Frances Lincoln Limited

Library of Congress Cataloging-in-Publication Data
French, Fiona.
    Anancy and Mr. Dry-Bone/Fiona French—1st U.S. ed.
        p.   cm.
    Summary: Anancy and Mr. Dry-Bone attempt to win the hand of the
      beautiful Miss Louise by making her laugh.
    ISBN 0-316-29298-2
    1. Anansi (Legendary character)—Juvenile fiction. [1. Anansi
      (Legendary character)—Fiction.] I. Title.
    PZ7.F8887An   1991
    [E]—dc20   90-53310

10 9 8 7 6 5 4 3 2 1

Published simultaneously in Canada
by Little, Brown & Company (Canada) Limited

Printed in Hong Kong

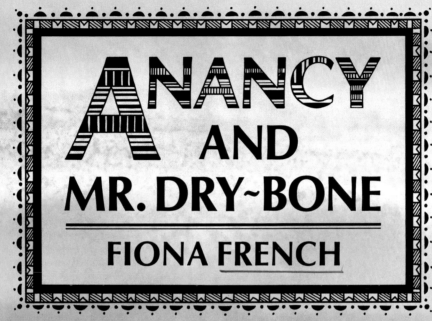

ANANCY
AND
MR. DRY-BONE

FIONA FRENCH

LITTLE, BROWN AND COMPANY
Boston   Toronto   London

Mr. Dry-Bone lived in a big house
at the top of a hill.
He was very rich and he wanted
to marry Miss Louise.

Anancy lived in a small house
at the foot of the hill.
He was very poor and he wanted to
marry Miss Louise as well.

Miss Louise lived on the other side of the hill.
She wasn't rich and she wasn't poor.
She was very clever and very, very beautiful.
But Miss Louise had never laughed
in her whole life, so the first man
who could make her laugh,
that was the one she'd marry.

Mr. Dry-Bone knocked on Miss Louise's
door. He was all dressed up in his
very best clothes.
"Good evening," he said.
"I've brought all my powerful
conjuring tricks and I'm going to
make you laugh."
"Well," said Miss Louise,
"this I've got to see."

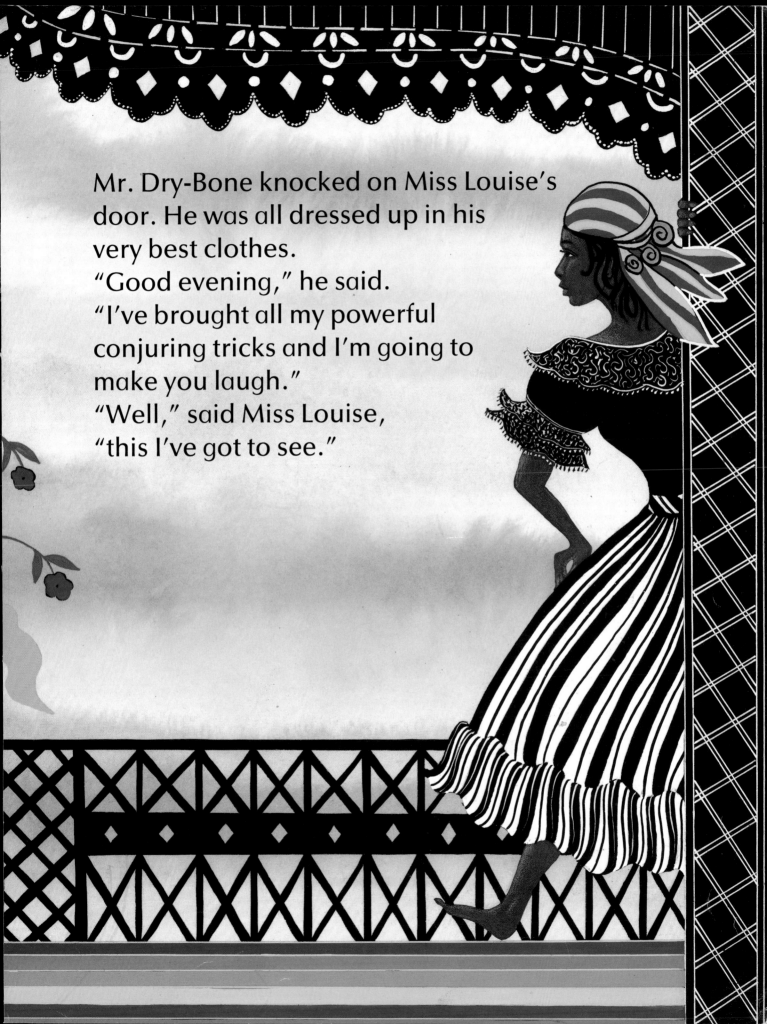

Mr. Dry-Bone turned himself into a bat
that flapped and a cat that spat;
he turned himself into a pig that honked
and a rabbit that did nothing.
But Miss Louise never smiled.

Mr. Dry-Bone turned somersaults and cartwheels and stood upside down on the ceiling.
But still Miss Louise never smiled.
Anancy said to himself,
"I can do better than that."

Anancy went to Tiger and said,
"Lend me your best evening suit,
I'm going to visit Miss Louise."
Tiger said, "My evening suit
is at the cleaners right now,
but you can borrow my jogging suit."

Anancy went to see Dog.
"Lend me your top hat,
I'm going to visit Miss Louise."
Dog said, "My top hat got
crushed the other day but
you can borrow my
hunting hat."

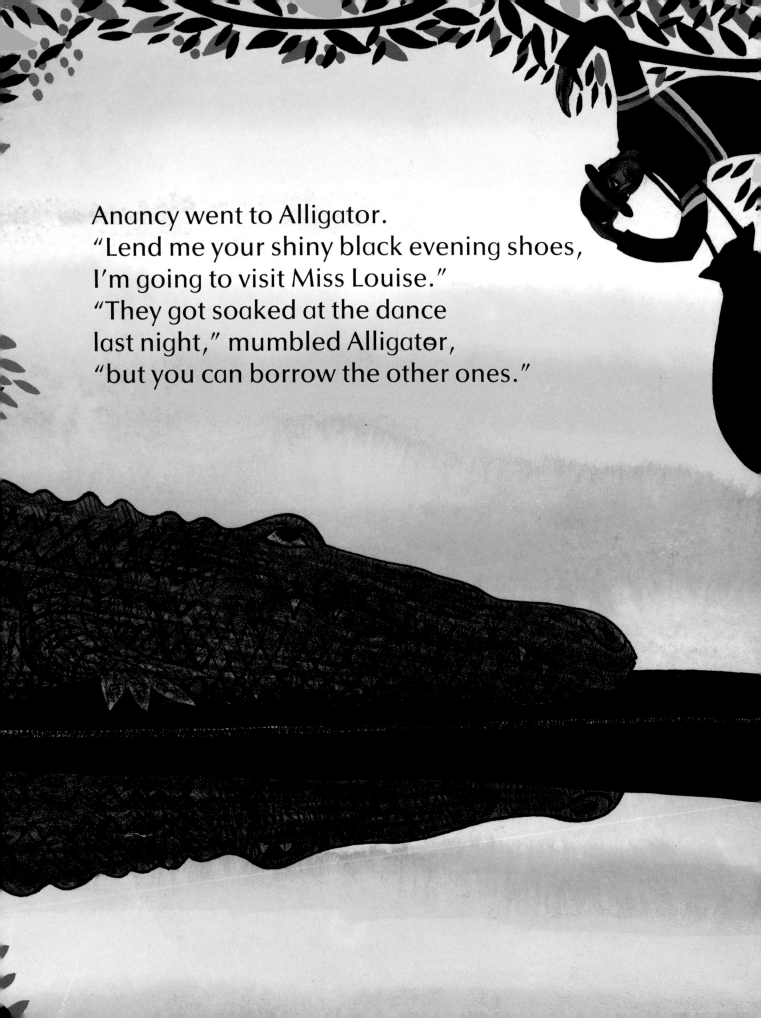

Anancy went to Alligator.
"Lend me your shiny black evening shoes,
I'm going to visit Miss Louise."
"They got soaked at the dance
last night," mumbled Alligator,
"but you can borrow the other ones."

Monkey swung through the trees
and called to Anancy,
"You'll need a tie when you
visit Miss Louise."

Parrot squawked and dropped
some feathers.
"Put these in your hunting hat, Anancy.
They'll look real good when you
visit Miss Louise."

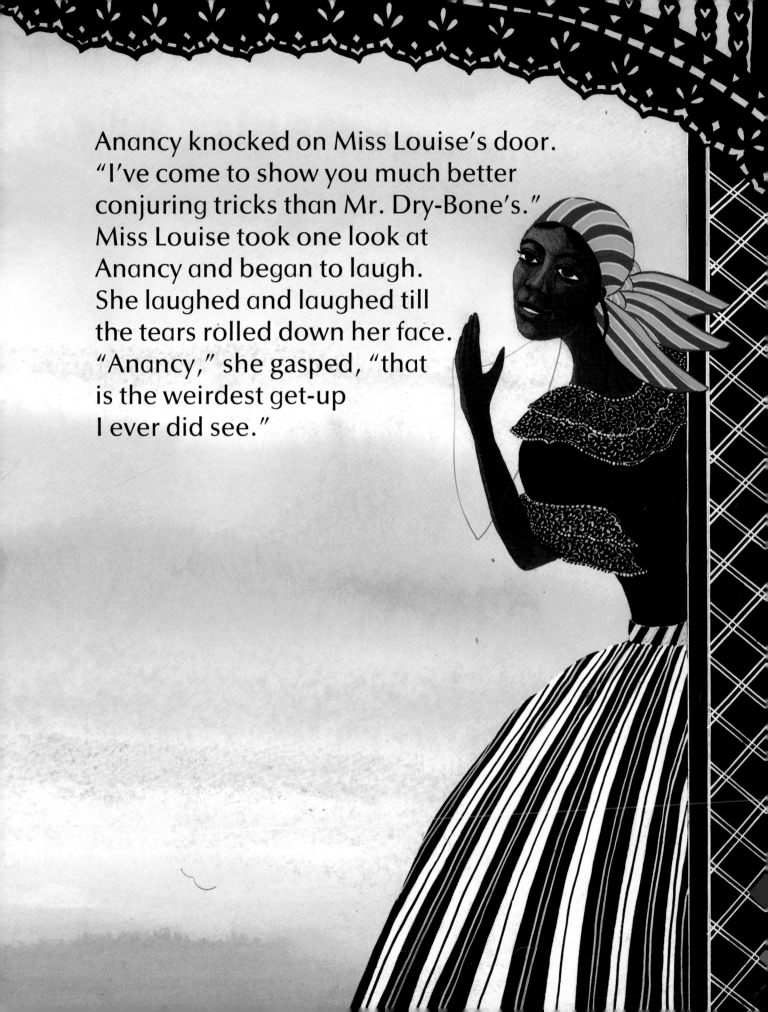

Anancy knocked on Miss Louise's door.
"I've come to show you much better
conjuring tricks than Mr. Dry-Bone's."
Miss Louise took one look at
Anancy and began to laugh.
She laughed and laughed till
the tears rolled down her face.
"Anancy," she gasped, "that
is the weirdest get-up
I ever did see."

Everyone laughed.
Even Mr. Dry-Bone.
"OK, you win," he said.

So Anancy married Miss Louise,
and they all lived happily
ever after.